D0811491

to teachers and parents

This is a LADYBIRD LEADER book, one of a series specially produced to meet the very real need for carefully planned *first information books* that instantly attract enquiring minds and stimulate reluctant readers.

The subject matter and vocabulary have been selected with expert assistance, and the brief and simple text is printed in large, clear type.

Children's questions are anticipated and facts presented in a logical sequence. Where possible, the books show what happened in the past and what is relevant today.

Special artwork has been commissioned to set a standard rarely seen in books for this reading age and at this price.

Full colour illustrations are on all 48 pages to give maximum impact and provide the extra enrichment that is the aim of all Ladybird Leaders.

Acknowledgment

The author and publishers wish to acknowledge the help given by Birmingham Dental School in the preparation of this book, and to thank Dr M E Corbett of the Department of Oral Pathology there for lending the reference used for the illustration of an elephant's tooth on page 30.

A Ladybird Leader

teeth

by Sandra Halford BDS

with illustrations by Vernon Mills, Jorge Nuñez
and Gerald Witcomb MSIAD

Photographs by John Moyes

Ladybird Books Ltd Loughborough 1978

This is a Ladybird book about teeth.
Ladybirds do not have teeth.
No insects have teeth.
They have hard mouth parts
called *mandibles.*

*head and
mouth parts
of a bee*

Plants make
their own food,
so they don't need teeth.

But animals need
to break food down
to feed.

For this
they need teeth.
The garden snail has
14,000 very small teeth.
They are in rows.
They look like a file.
They break down plant food.

5

The origin of teeth

All life began in the sea.

Teeth developed from small spines on the skin.

These were called *dermal denticles*.

In the mouth they formed teeth.

This shark has small spines
over its skin.
In its mouth are rows of sharp teeth.

Teeth tell us a lot about animals: Herbivores

Herbivores have long jaws
and a big mouth with
a long row of molars.

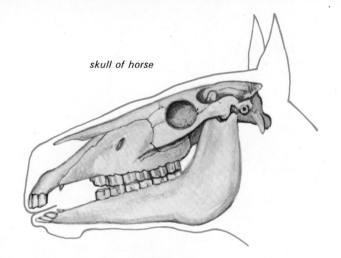

skull of horse

Herbivores eat plants, which they must chew and grind up.

This is why they have broad blunt teeth.

9

Carnivores

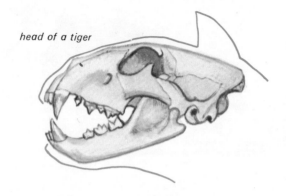

head of a tiger

Carnivores are meat eaters —
they eat other animals.
They slice meat
and swallow it in one piece.

In prehistoric times,
the sabre-toothed tiger
hunted big herbivores for food.

It had two long curved canine teeth
which grew downwards
from the upper jaw.

The teeth easily killed animals
and tore the meat from the bones.

Teeth in prehistoric animals

The flying reptiles had
sharp pointed teeth.

They ate fish.

The teeth pointed forwards.

Fish are slippery.

Sharp teeth helped the reptile
to hold the fish.

Teeth for fighting

The male hippopotamus
uses his huge tusks
for fighting
and to dig up plants.
He uses his molars
to chew plant food.

Snakes

Poisonous snakes have a hole
or a groove in their teeth.

Poison passes down the hole
when the snake bites a victim.

Non-poisonous snakes have teeth
which point backwards
into the mouth,
so that when they seize their prey,
it cannot escape.

Rodents

Rodents gnaw
with their strong *incisor* teeth.

Squirrels can bite
through nut shells.

The incisors keep on growing
as the crown of the tooth
is worn down.

Beavers

Beavers can bite their way
through trees
with their chisel-like front teeth.

They have been known
to fell trees 45 centimetres thick.

The bark and leaves
provide their food.

Omnivores

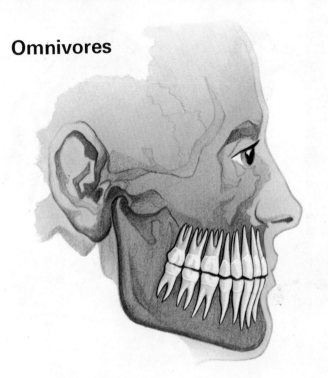

Human beings are *omnivores.*
This means that we eat
both meat and plants.
We have teeth at the front
to cut and slice food.
We have teeth at the back
to grind and chew.

Fibrous foods

Beavers, camels and pandas
all eat fibrous foods
which help to keep their teeth clean.

Camels eat the thorny shrubs
that grow in the desert.

Bamboo shoots provide the panda with the bulk of his food.

Human teeth

Our front teeth are called *incisors*.
They are for biting.
Next to these are the *canines*.
They have sharp points
to slice and tear food.
Our back teeth are called *molars*.
They are for chewing.

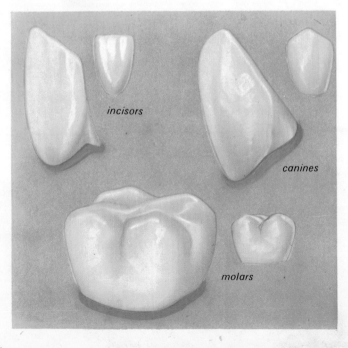

incisors

canines

molars

We only have two sets of teeth
all our lives,
so we have to look after them.
When our baby (*milk*) teeth fall out,
they are followed
by our permanent teeth.
Many other animals
have two sets of teeth too.
Sharks and crocodiles
grow new teeth
as the old ones wear away.

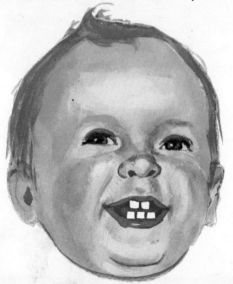

Teeth grow in the jaw bone.
The upper jaw is part of the skull.
The lower jaw moves up and down.
Teeth of the two jaws bite
against each other.

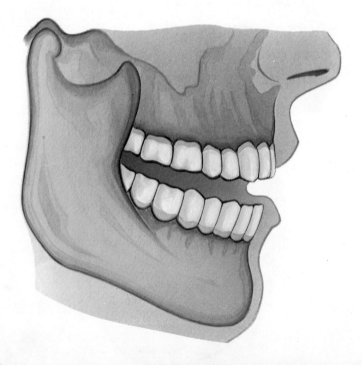

Our teeth fit into deep cups
in the bone.

The cups are called sockets.

The part of the tooth in the socket
is the root.

The crown is the part we can see
in the mouth.

If our teeth are cut in half
(like an apple is cut in half),
we can see the layers of the tooth.

Enamel covers the crown.

It is the hardest part of the body.

Cementum covers the root.

Dentine forms the main part
of the tooth.

In the middle is the *pulp cavity*,
where there are nerves
and blood vessels.

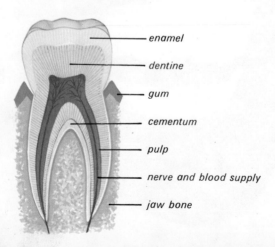

enamel

dentine

gum

cementum

pulp

nerve and blood supply

jaw bone

Animal teeth

Horses have molars with open roots.

Rodents have incisors
with open roots.

Teeth with open roots
keep on growing
as they are worn down.

The roots of our teeth are pointed.

Our teeth do not go on growing
as they wear away.

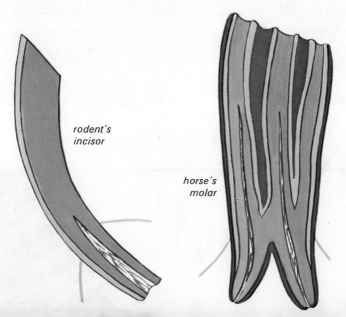

rodent's
incisor

horse's
molar

The elephant has the biggest teeth
in the world.

The crown of the molar
is made of enamel, dentine
and cementum next to each other.

These three are not all as hard
as each other.

Cementum and dentine
wear away quickest.

Enamel is much harder.

Ridges of enamel grind up plant food.

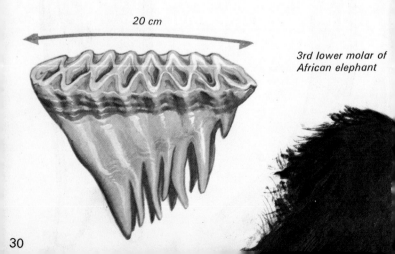

20 cm

3rd lower molar of
African elephant

At London Zoo one day
Guy the Gorilla was ill.
He would not eat his food.
He was sick and unhappy.
Some of his teeth had holes in.
They were decayed,
and he was in pain.

Why did Guy's teeth decay?

Children visiting the zoo
had given Guy all sorts of food
with sugar in it –
buns, biscuits, sweets
and ice cream.
The veterinary surgeon at the zoo
had to take out the bad teeth.
Nowadays visitors are not allowed
to feed the animals
at the zoo.

Bears living in the wild
eat a lot of food rich in sugar.

Bears love honey.

A lot of them have decay
in their teeth.

Plaque

Every day a film called *plaque*
grows on our teeth and gums.

We cannot see it at first.

It contains millions of germs.

If left there
we begin to see it on our teeth,
especially next to the gums.

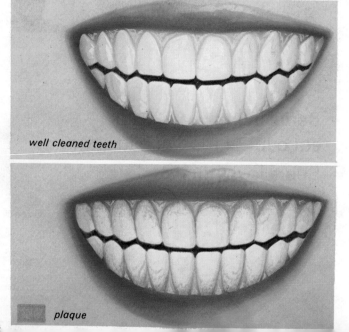

well cleaned teeth

plaque

Why does sugar cause tooth decay?

The germs in the plaque
change sugar to acid,
which lies in the plaque
next to the enamel.

The acid starts to dissolve enamel
under the plaque.

The enamel becomes softer,
and germs then start to eat away
the softer part of the tooth,
leading to decay.

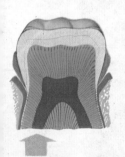

*plaque forms on
the enamel*

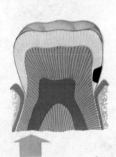

*the acid eats into
the enamel and
decay begins*

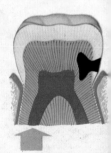

*decay extends
into the dentine*

Cave men had almost no decay
in their teeth.

The Romans had
a lot more tooth decay
than the Anglo Saxons.

The Romans ate softer food
and used honey
to sweeten some foods.

Queen Elizabeth the first
had very bad teeth.

One of her bishops
had a tooth taken out.

She was then brave enough
to have a bad tooth taken out too.

How can you look after your teeth and gums?

Crocodiles have many teeth.

They cannot clean the teeth themselves.

A little bird cleans their teeth.

It picks food
from the crocodile's teeth,
while the crocodile is sleeping.

Centuries ago
when there were no toothbrushes
or toothpaste,
people made simple toothbrushes
out of twigs.

They used salt or ashes as toothpaste.

We are luckier.
We have proper toothbrushes
and toothpaste.

Brushing

To help to keep healthy teeth,
we must brush them every day.

We should brush them after breakfast
and before going to bed,
and if possible after every meal.

We need to brush all parts
of the teeth:
front, back and chewing surfaces.
You should ask your dentist
the best way to do this.

This is one method you can use.

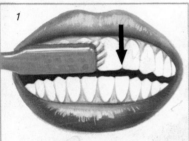

1

*brush top teeth
downwards from gums to tip*

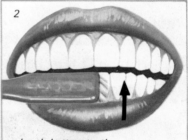

2

*brush bottom teeth
upwards from gums to tip*

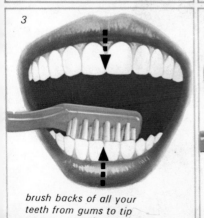

3

*brush backs of all your
teeth from gums to tip*

4

*brush biting surfaces with
a backward and forward action*

Toothpaste is important
for cleaning the teeth.

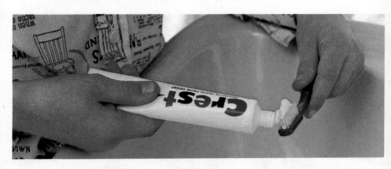

It helps the brush
to remove the plaque.

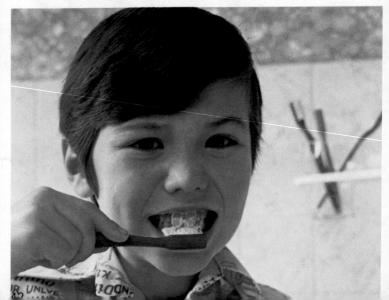

Dental scientists have proved
that toothpastes
with *fluoride* in them are best.

Fluoride is a special substance
that strengthens tooth enamel
against decay.

Dentists advise that a toothbrush
should be replaced
every eight to ten weeks.

Regular brushing
with a good toothbrush
will remove plaque.

We must try not to eat sugary food between meals.

Remember, too many sweets made Guy's teeth bad!

Healthy diet

Foods such as nuts,
apples and cheese
are much better for our teeth
than sweet things.

Animals need dentists

This is a veterinary surgeon.

He is an animal doctor –
often called a vet for short.

A dental surgeon is called a dentist
in the same way.

A vet is also an animal dentist.

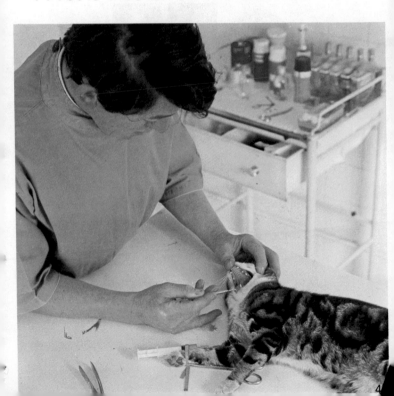

An animal at a vet's surgery
usually behaves well.
The vet is its friend.
He will help the animal
to get better.

We need dentists

Dentists are our friends.

We should visit our dentist
every four months.

Dentists can help us
to keep our teeth strong
and healthy.

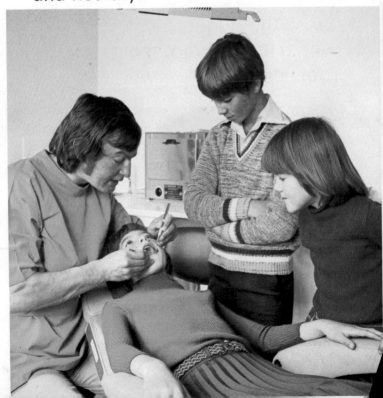

How to have healthy teeth

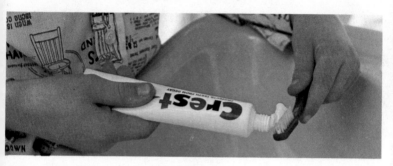

1 Brush thoroughly
   with a fluoride toothpaste
   every day.

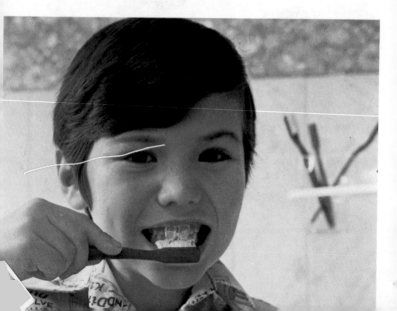

2 Don't eat sugary snacks
  between meals.
  Eat nuts, apples
  and cheese instead.

3 Visit your dentist
  every four months for a check-up.

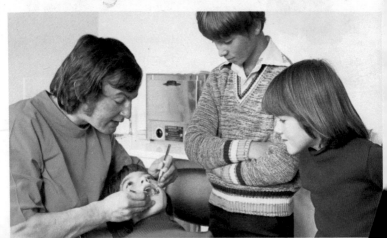

Index